Ruby's
Reunion Day Dinner

Ruby's Reunion Day Dinner

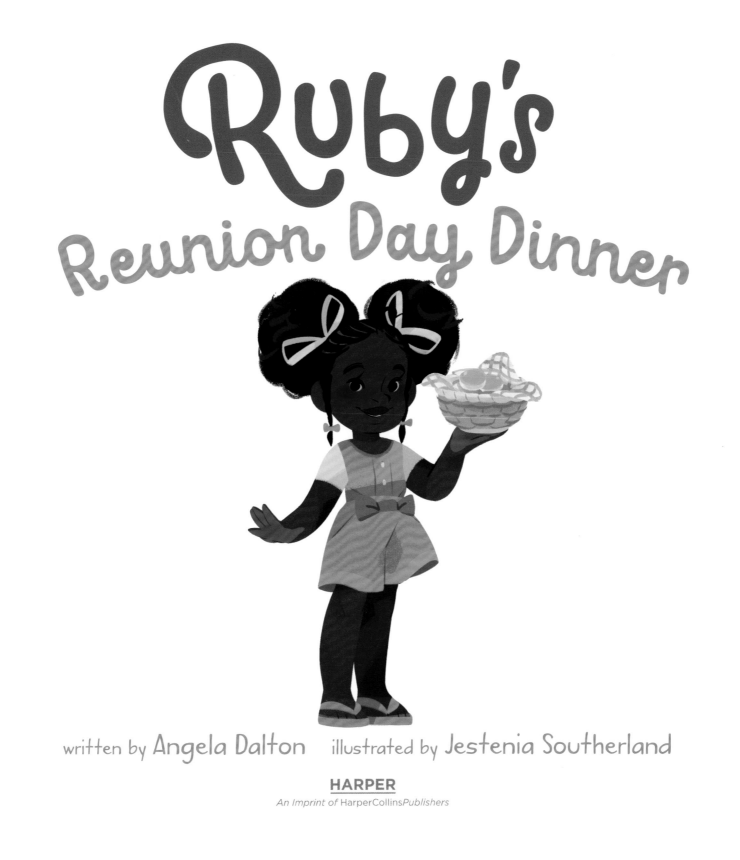

written by Angela Dalton   illustrated by Jestenia Southerland

HARPER
An Imprint of HarperCollinsPublishers

Library of Congress Control Number: 2020950476

ISBN 978-0-06-301574-6

The artist used Photoshop to create the digital illustrations for this book.

Typography by Rachel Zegar

21 22 23 24 25   RTLO   10 9 8 7 6 5 4 3 2 1

❖

First Edition

For my momma: Thank you for teaching
me that the food you make and share should
always be served with a side of love.
—A.D.

To my family, whose support and
delicious meals are invaluable.
—J.S.

Grocery bags rustle, pots and pans clatter, and the room quakes with laughter as my family gathers in Grammy and Pop-Pop's kitchen to make Reunion Day dinner.

And not just any dinner—a soul food dinner.

Every auntie, uncle, and cousin has a special something they cook and share once a year, what Daddy calls their "signature dish." Everyone but me.

"Momma," I ask, "what can I make this year?"
"What do you have in mind, baby?"
I shrug.

"You sure you're big enough to help,
Lil' Bit?" asks Auntie Billie, teasing me.
"I'm sure," I say, but I'm not.

"You'll think of something."
Momma pecks my forehead
with a kiss and gets back to
her stirring.

I watch my family bustle about and think, *There has to be something that's just right for me.*

Peering over the counter, I see: Momma's gooey peach cobbler bubbling up the sides of her favorite baking dish, the golden, crispy crown of Daddy's perfect mac 'n' cheese, the streaky unmixed layers of Grammy's hush puppy batter.

"Can I mix the batter, Grammy?" I ask.

"Why, this mixer is bigger than you, Lil' Bit. Next year, baby."

Wandering to the stove, I hear: the crack and sizzle of chicken and catfish frying up in Pop-Pop's iron skillet, the sharp whistle of red beans boiling in Uncle Mope's pressure cooker, the slow babbling of collard greens simmering in Auntie Patty's large stockpot.

"Can I stir the greens, Auntie Patty?" I ask.

"Stove's too hot—you might hurt yourself. Next year, Lil' Bit."

Sneaking sniffs around the food table, I smell: the sugary scent of marshmallows melting on top of Cousin Irene's sweet candied yams, the spicy perfume of cloves from Uncle Red's glazed maple ham, the reek of onions Uncle G's preparing to fry—they may be tasty, but they sure do stink!

"Can I help cut the onions, Uncle G?"
I look up to his face.
"I know." I sigh. "Maybe next year."

My mouth waters as I head outside, just thinking about: the zing of Auntie Lena's pickled okra that crunch when you bite them, the tang of Cousin Tee-Tee's homemade hot sauce that stings my tongue just right, the perk of sweet juice from Auntie Billie's grilled corn.

I sit on the back steps. Head bowed, shoulders slouched.

"Whoo, kitchen's hot, but the grill out here's hotter!" says Auntie Billie, wiping the sweat trickling down her brow as she turns the meats and veggies.

That's when I see it—the perfect job for me!

"Auntie Billie!" I say,
running up to her.
  "Now, Lil' Bit, you know
you're too young to mess
with this grill."

"Not that," I say,
pointing behind
her. "That!"

Picking lemons
so yellow they make
my eyes squint, I press
and roll them hard to loosen
the juice before Uncle G helps me cut and
squeeze them.

Then I measure the "just-right" scoop of brown sugar to make a lemonade tart enough to pucker my lips into a heart shape.

After letting it chill in the fridge, I place my jar on the table next to the rest of our Reunion Day dinner.

"Looks like you found your signature dish," Daddy says as he and my family drink with sweet relief from the heat.

"You outdid yourself with this lemonade, Ruby," Auntie Billie says between slurps. "You promise to make it again next year?"

I smile, hearing her say my real name. "Yes! And it'll be even better!"